TWILIGHT DIARY

FANTASY-FICTION, VAMPIRES, WITCHS, DARK MAGIC, ADULT-FICTION

AF569195

A. G. MORNINGSTAR

Copyright © A. G. Morningstar
All Rights Reserved.

This book has been self-published with all reasonable efforts taken to make the material error-free by the author. No part of this book shall be used, reproduced in any manner whatsoever without written permission from the author, except in the case of brief quotations embodied in critical articles and reviews.

The Author of this book is solely responsible and liable for its content including but not limited to the views, representations, descriptions, statements, information, opinions and references ["Content"]. The Content of this book shall not constitute or be construed or deemed to reflect the opinion or expression of the Publisher or Editor. Neither the Publisher nor Editor endorse or approve the Content of this book or guarantee the reliability, accuracy or completeness of the Content published herein and do not make any representations or warranties of any kind, express or implied, including but not limited to the implied warranties of merchantability, fitness for a particular purpose. The Publisher and Editor shall not be liable whatsoever for any errors, omissions, whether such errors or omissions result from negligence, accident, or any other cause or claims for loss or damages of any kind, including without limitation, indirect or consequential loss or damage arising out of use, inability to use, or about the reliability, accuracy or sufficiency of the information contained in this book.

Made with ♥ on the Notion Press Platform
www.notionpress.com

ꝒꝒꝒ

I REALLY GET A CHANCE TO BE NORMAL KID

A.G. MORNINGSTAR

YOUR AFFECTIONATE ANIMA AMOROSOA

A. G. Morningstar

KIERNAN SHIPKA

Kiernan credo che le storie d'amore piu' vere non finicano mai. Ti amo cosi tanto piccola mia, quella bellezza diabolica e ill diavolo sono la stessa cosa.

Sei amore

A.G. Morningstar.

My Dear kiernan shipka,

I wrote this story for you, but when i began it. I had not realized that girl i saw in my dream grow quicker than books. As a result you are already too old for fairy tales, and by the time it is printed and bound you will be older still. but some day you will be old enough to start reading fairy tales again. I shall probably be there to hear and too old to understand a words you say, but i shall still be.

A.G. Morningstar

Contents

Foreword

IT *were all could one do take a pen and contribute a character sketch or more interesting than that writer himslef . To me, lucky chance if anything in this world. some things are worth the splurge . The following lines written with a sincere desire , but this is because it has seemed to me necessary to state how life appears at its most serious beginning .*

Preface

I fever the story of any man's Adventure's in the world were worth making publick, and were acceptale.

the wonders of this man's life exceed all that(he thinks) is to be found extant.,

Life itslef is only a vision, a dream . Nothing exists save empty space , and you! and your are but a thought. The rarest of treasures are found in darkest of place, let lucifer gudie you to a place of great knowledge where god cannot even go. Devil and I get along just fine.

Acknowledgements

A.G. Morningstar is the single writer of weired... HIS achievement lies not so much in his influence as in the enduring qualities of his finest work.

I REPEAT TO YOU, My Narcissim that your inquistion is fruitless. Detain me here forever if you will, confine or execute me if you must be the victim to propitate the illusion you call justice; But i can say no mare than i have said already . Everything that i remember , i have told you with perfect candour. When you read these hastily scraweled pages you may gusses, though never fully realise, it is only because of the dark cloud which come over my mind-that cloud and the nebulous nature of horrors which brought upon me to her.

[" O DARLING WHEN LITTLE GIRLS WANTED TO BE LILITH. THERE I WANTED TO BE BLOOD SUCKING VAMPIRE"] - A. G. Morningstar

Prologue

Hey reader, i'm A.G.Morningstar what's the matter? are you afraid of vampires amd witches? hee he, no need to worry , i'm not staying for dinner, i'm here to tell you story of sweet little girl. I could feel the sense shivering touch of the venis on my throat and the razar-sharp teeth on kiernan shipka. A narmol girl with supernatural powers. she is unware of her destiny she bron to fullfil and now on 16th birthday, her life takes 180 degree turn. where she finds herslef is hybird girl half-vampire and half-witch, satan searches for bride a woman named kiernan shipka. as he wants her to bear his child and destroy the world. what will happen? when she discover her true identy?

ONE

TWILIGHT ECLIPES

Once upon a time in december 1960 in twilight eclipes. A place separated, from human civilistion magical mirror wall , there was another deep forest where magical creature lived like Goblins, Elves, Pixes, Faires were almost extinct and lived in hiding from the majorty " THE VAMPIRES " . Vampire council members of which comprised vampire sorcers, scorcer who had tured into vampire by making the contract with pure-blood vampires. Werewolves and witches who rivalled them strengths amd magical abilites, their sworn enemies lived separately between the magical world and human world at the periphery of forest marking their territories.

placed on high mountain was an old house of Dracula castle. the castle glowed with eclipes light that night for the celebration of the Vampire Kings birthday. the sound of the celebration echoed throughout, the entire forest. Even the hidden creatures came out to celebrate their kings birth anniversary dancing along the path. the castle was loud with cheer. All the Noble Vampire lined up to wish him, all the girls awaited his presence, they were all glitttered up to impress him. Tonight he was going to choose his Queen.

a carriage made its way to castle , hearing the creak of the wheel . All the creatures ran back into their hiding place . The castle enormous gate opened for it to enter, it stopped in the front of the entrance.

COUNT OF DRACULA CASTLE

Look at those fools. we arrived a little late and they dared to think thaey had achance against my lady? the girl helped her missters with her dress as she stepped out of the carriage. thats difference you fool those uselees fellows are supposed to arrive earler to glorify ours. said the other one.

those low lives need to learn their place, the Queen has already been decided only the off for official announment remains. once the door opened a powerful pressence penetrated the warm atmosphere. All eyes were down and the servants practically lied on the floor while the nobles bowed down to her presence.

Nyla spencer made her way inside the castle ; She was the daughter of head of the Vampire council and most suitable candidate for the Vampire Queen. At another part of the castle , there was restless ; the King had disappeared from his own birthady party. his misstress dispached a search team for him.

Asher Dracula was fifth king of the vampire worlsd, the king reigend for thousands of years until they found someone more worthy of the throne, be their son or daughter/ grands or further down the line . Asher Dracula ancestor ruled for 3000yrs until finally he was born dark powers which kept him away from him and all his life he faced loneliness. The only one that enters his world, piercing the surrounding darkness, was Diana Woods. she belong to a powerful ancient with witch coven ruled by female witchcraft; she was born with brithmark of the moon, making her the female witch choosen by the moon godess herself.

when Asher Dracula reached serpent falls, their meeting place he found Diana Woods staring at the full moon; the pixes were dancing around her, he smiled as collided right into her an stabilising themselves the scoldedone another, then they all immediately bowed dowm to their King, Diana still didnt noticed his presence, he gestured them to leave quietly ,They obilged and took off; He the approached his beloved quietly and hugged her from behind.

Happy Brithday! she smiled as she leaned her head back. He pressed a kiss to her nape of her neck, licking the mark on her . she shivered at the sensation.

How? i thought you were still busy staring at the twilight eclipses moon. he groaned breathing her scent.

She turned to him and leaned in to catch his lips in a brief kiss. he pulled her in a deep kiss, parting he rested his forehead against her.

I can't do anything about this jealousy of yours." she smiled , caressing his cheeks.

I dont ever get it, whats with you and the moon? he rolled his eyes. forget that here, he extened his hand.

What?" she raised her brows.

Whats with that look? do you can get away with it? my birthday present. where is it? he inquired.

She then held his hand and guieded them to her belly.

He frowend this is that...

She nodded.

The ground shook. dont lose it , idiot! she slapped his back as his powers created turbulence in nature.

I LOVE YOU. He picked her up amd spun around. thank you this the best gift ever . slowly lowering her to, ground, he claimed her lips in a sweet kiss.

His happniess was short-lived when he heard the footsteps from miles away,; Damn!, he swore under his breath.

I've discussed the propsal with the council. We won't hvae to sneak in the dark to.meet eachother, very i'll make you my queen . you me and our child, we'll live happily like any othr family. for real? HE smiled at her .

Is it really possible? this dream, can we live it for real? thousands of yrs of enmity. can we erase it? she questioned.

Our clans nad coven didn't clash in ancient times. didn't you tellme stories of the ancient times, when our clan and coven lived in harmony with each other.

Yes' but those stories were tens of thousands of years ago, no wthey're enemies hunting each other , thats what they are for, i'm sacared they will hunt us down like others who dared to love oppsite? will our child be able to...

Shh... . He sealed his lips with slow and sensual kiss on her lips. Breaking apart he looked into her eys . we'll bring the change . I am the vampire king and you're my queen. We have the support from you're , one the most powerful among others. We'll have our dream turned into reality. Vampire and witche both will come togethr again , there won't be any casualties , i promise. He sealed it with a kiss on her lips. when she opened her eyes, he was gone.

I'll be waiting. She whispered into space.

SERPENT FALLS

TWO

HERITAGE LINE

The year passed away like a season as the moon shining bent through the moon-light but not in the darkness.

In-1961 somewhere in Transylvanian.

St. Grave Desire

Hollow tops is a mountian in chruch-land pinnacle a hidden mansion the hell sundry. St. Grave desire is a deep hidden graveyad from muggle is loacted in the forest of gentle apple forest

Asher , who was seated outside the room with flowers, as soon the doctor came he stood and went walking towards the doctor slowly and he asked. Doctor is everything alright and what about my child, doctor looked at the man in sorrow. The man looking in some hope , the doctor im sorry Asher you're... but before that. At once the nurse came running behind the doctor screaming , doctor doctor ... the old nurse took a deep breath and said. Doctor please you have to a look into. MR. Asher was feeling nervous about their action. After sometime the doctor came back outside the room and looked MR.Asher congratulations your father now for the baby girl from the blessing from Dark Lord; All at once there were big thunderstroms and its started raining, from a long distance there was noise screaming.

MR.Asher was stunned by hearing this from doctor and he started to cry in symathic and he asked doctor ; Doctor can i see my wife?. The doctor said, yes you can please go head, doctor showing his hand towards the door to his wife and his baby girl.

A car came halt and old nun stepped out of the car, with rosary in her hand, the dark forset echoed numberous footsteps.

The chase was long, but they needed to hunt them. One vampire commaded.

we dont follow you're orders. one of the werewovles growled in response.

Whe little creatureon the way crawled inside their hosue and had their doors shut.

There is no time to complain, we must find them! wtich said.

Groups were formed and sent in different direction.

One vampire ran head of the werewolves, the other one paced by their side mocking them for slow pace nd then zoomed ahead.

How dare they? the werewolf growled and was about to move to hunt down for their audacity.

Stop the witch transformed into young lady, ingnore her and focus on finding that bitch. It's all because of her, she has disgraced the Dark Lord, find her and kill her along with her baby.

The vampire and werewolves entered the mansion through the window .

The old nun seated on the couch and MR. Asher was looking at her face in faer. MR. Asher walked towards the ild nun. The nun chanting prayers.

I came here to help you MR. Asher . Said the nun.

No i dont need anyone around me. Said mr. Asher

The witch entered the room with her big nails grown amd went closer to the baby.

Here you come to me, you're mummy....is fast alseep... Witch whispered.

The vampire and werewolves entred the room.

Diana opended her eyes and pushed the witch and with her might force and carried her baby and ran into the woods.

Haah... haah.. Diana screamed, the witch chanted the spell on her. Diana ran with all her might but she could'nt lose the vampire and werewolves behind her, she was weak because of the childbirth, the labour was hard and soon after they were being chased, if she could turn into her witch form, she thought as she hid behind a large tree.

She heard hundreds of footsteps coming closer to them. This is not good, i'll have to distract them. She placed her new born baby on the ground . be good and wait for mama to come for you. She whispered to her child as she took out a necklace that had a small bottle tied on it. She sprinkled the water from it on her child. This will mask you scent. She whispered.

Diana shut her eyes and tired to communicate, Asher as she tired to telepathy . Asher i call upon you to come before me. The only one who had powers to throw them off without touching them.

Sorry i was late, she heard him inside her mind.

where are you?

Asher said. Diana, i am right here!! Open your eyes

Diana woods opens her eyes and hugs. Asher tightly in constant fear.

Hide somewhere safe. i'll come after handling them. Come back to us safe. She whispered dashed back to her child.

HUSH, everthing is going to fine now. Papa is here, he'll come to us soon. She kissed her baby and held her close lets get you somewhere safe.

Just as she was about to move she heard someone move swiftly behind her. The witch swifitly towards them.

It's the dead-end. Diana woods... one of the werewolf scoffed at her as he walked towards them.

Stay away; Cain , she shouted.

Guess what? we dont take your oreders anymore, diana. Witch appeared beside her .

Let us go.

Hand over the baby and i swear you'll be spared. The witch said slowly appraching her.

Over my dead body!!

we gotta get out of here, she held her baby close to her chest nd went invisible and ran from there,

Diana!! she heard her husband.

We're here, Asher. She said called out him

I'm so glad you guys are fine. He smiled weakly.

What's wrong? she frowned

Nothing , lets get out of here, he tired to move but fell on the ground. His face was pale and he was severely injured his wounds were gaping.

Asher?! she shouted she had never seen him like that, his injury always healed on its own he was invincible.

They injected me with something, he winced in pain sensing the danger lurking around he whispered. Listen you need to get out here.

We.. we need to get out of here. She cupped his cheeks

Just then one vampire appeared, your majesty. He knelt in front of his king.

Listen , diana he'll take you smewhere safe where vampires and werewovles wont be able to reach you guys. Asher assured her.

I'm not leaving you behind . She shouted tears filled her eyes, i'm not.

It's not time to be stubborn, you guys aren't safe here. He scolded her.

you're not either. she aruged.

I'm the Vampire King, remember? he cupped her cheeks and rested his forehead against she , please listen to me once in a while.

Fine we'll send our child with him but i'm staying with you. She told him

You know that's not possible, our child won't be able to surive alone this our heritage line. She have tremendous amount of powers, she needs you to guide her. Asher argued.

He took his daughter in his arms, finallly he could look at her face, my pride! He planted a soft kisson her forehead, he took her little hands into his his and kissed them. She'll do what we couldn't , he whispered as he took at his wife, she was a child prophecy destined to bring the lords of earh together, destined to rule over earth his gaze shifted back at child. Sorry that papa can't come with you but promise to return to ypu soon.

Handing her over to her mother , he held his tears back; Now go. He stood up turing back to them.

No please don't do this to me. She begged

He tured to her and pulled her in a hug , after this ends i swear i'll come back to you. He kissed her in tears.

Promise me.

I Promise , he sealed it with kiss on a her lips, now go

Dinna Woods

I love you, he whispered before he teleported them to end of the forest.

I love you as she whispered in the air, seeing the moon.

THREE

DECEMBER SNOW

Sixteen-years later - FOXBURGH

"Mom! im getting late, a girl shouting as she tied her long hair into pony. where's my lucky Red drees?" she shouted throwing the clothes out of the wardrobe.

"on the bed" she heard her mom shout from downstaris.

"where are my lucky shoes? she shouted again as put on her dress. Right at your doorstep. Her mother replied.

she opened the door to find them, putting them on. She hurried down the staris picking her bag" Okay bye mom, love ya. She give her a flying kiss and rushed to door, but before could open her door she felt hug on her arm. " Hang on a minute!. Her mother pulled her from behind.

"Is it necessary for you to go? Her mother heaved a deep sigh. " My dear overprotective mother!. I'm not five years-old kid that'll get lost. I'm turning sixteen tomorrow and i'm not going to moon, it's two hours drive by car. I'm just going on a trip with my friends, i promise i'll take care myself and return home before night happy.

"Tch she clicked her tonuge as she saw her mom face clouded with worry. I've also got your favourite bodygurad with me, remember? she tried to pacify her by mentioning her reliable mlae friends. Just then they heard the honking of the car. Now can i go before they wake up the entire neighbourhood with that sound? she cupped her mother face.

" Of course mamma its December snow,. Kiernan said take care bye love and kissed her mother cheeks.

What's this? you're into it again? Didnt you already read it like thousand of times? she asked as soon as he got into the car and saw her friend holding the Twilight Diary .

Oh come on! Don't underestimate my love Abba i can read it for another thousand times! her eyes had heart.

Of course you're favourite neighbour again! Jasmine rolled her eyes. can't help it! jasmine a 24 yrs old, was my senior in high school, happy go lucky girl and of course a big a fan of Abba, ever since her high school. they had been friends since high school and there wasn't a singlr day without Abba, where she didnt speak of his myth.

"Kiernan dont you remember what happend inthe bathroom? jasmine mocking. The car halted and impact threw the two of them in front. What the hell Ray! Kiernan shouted at her friend who was in driver seat. Ray her friend since high school.

"Give me break already! you guys are waering my ears out!"

Yeah, poor you lia clicked her tounge from the passenger seat,. Lia, kiernan best friend since high school.

Thanks lia , " Ray muttered as lips preesd together in tight line. Lia do you know, lucy was feeling guily towards me in middle school years.

Stop talking stupidly! Kiernan mocked jasmine.

Shut up! Don't ruin my moment! You vampire! jasmine galred at her.

" Exuse me! Don't you dare me call me bloodsucking monster! Kiernan scoffed.

Yes! your decision made my life easier fot you take Abba off.

What are you talking about? Kiernan rised middle finger at jasmine.

ÞÞÞ

KIERNAN SHIPKA

FOUR
HIGH SCHOOL

Our first class went by as uneventful as could be. It was maths class and its was extremely boring,

nevertheless we pulled through and went to ur next class ' history however,just before class i made a vist to the toilet where saw sight. I opened the door to find jasmine giving someone who i recognised as the new guy blowjob inthe girls bathroom.

"Oh my gosh!" I yelled , horrified at the sight in fornt of me. Neither behaved aas though they saw me and continued until the guy released all over her face.

I watched as she smiled and licked her lips before washing her face clean with water. "Later baby 'jasmine said blowing him kiss before leaving.

I watched the whole scene with a jaw down before eventually bringing my eyes back to him who was leaning against the wall with a satisfied smirk on his face.

"Oh my god " I yelled staring at him" What the heck was that.

Instead of apologising, he scowled at me and asked " Don't you have any manners at all ?

"Exuse me?!

"You heard me, didn;t your parents teach you any manners? if you wanted in could you just indicated.

"First of all, you're in high school. Secondly what the hell are you saying? I wasn't the one getting blowjob in girls bathroom.

"Okay...what the heck was that? I asked myslef as i stared at the door, unable to get gross just plain gross.

"Um excuse me . butbyou're on my seat. I said gently tapping his shoulder.

he looked upand groaned."Oh its you".

"whatever dipshit! youre on my seat.

"I don't see anyone here so no".

"This my seat. I sit here every timeinthe class".

"That doesn't amke it yours now does it?

I sighed im really not in the mood for all this um..."

Abba'

" Yeah Abba so could you please get up and find another seat?

"No you find another seat. im sitting right here and there's nothing you can do tochange that...unless ypou would like to sit on my lap, of course" winked at her

"EWW! I replied shivering.

"Miss Lara, could you please take your seat?

Class is about to begin," The teacher said alerting me to her persence. Abba snickered and i fought the urge to himas i took a seat a few charis away from him.

"Shit!" I thought as i glared daggers at back of his head for reminder of the class.

"I'm so dead mom's ging to kill me . It's also 11 PM! Look at the number missed class! I told you we should leave earlier". Kiernan shouted as she got out of the car.

"How that not my fault? The car broke down, remember? Ray said in his defence.

"Come on,"Lia hugged her her best friend tring to clam down,." It's your B'DAY in few hours cheer up.

Okay but i have to go home before twelve but it's already late now.

KIERNAN SHIPKA

FIVE

HAPPY DEATH DAY

Kiernan coudn't fathom what was happening as she had been out with her friends..The plan was to leave in the morning,because of the car break down." But she has to be there before sunrise. That she needed a familier soul around her. Her mother,so she booked a car for a rental at the hotel where her friends were staying.

She was driving for an hour now highway through NGO,"may be i'v," Her GPS had let her down tonight and the engine was a little stiff because of the cold weather.

The road had been snowing heavily. She could baarely see the path,Blace ice everywhere. Ideally kiernan would have taken a halt, but the place looked haunted with barely any cars along the narrow lanes that she decided againt. "This is part of the woods where everything usually goes wrong in horror movies.

As she thought about it,fear crept into her veins adding to all the others unusual things that were already happening inside her. The terrain was so bad that driving along straight was becoming a challenge. But she was too scared to stop here,in the loneliest,most deserted part of the highway.

Kiernan picked up her phone while trying hard to steer,so she could inform her mother.Mom would be terrified if she knew,it's better i tell her .... She thought out loud trying to juggle the wheel with one hand and operating her phone with other.".... Ugh.

All of a sudden,she lost control of the vehcile. The tires skid on the black ice and before she could brace herself,the car spun and rammed out of the lane,directly into the trees.

Her phone fell right between the pedals,"on god no,no,no oh god."

Her body was aching,her head spinning,her vision was blurring out,yet she kept trying to save herself. With full force,she hit the pedal with her foot,and it turns out it was the gas. The car accelerated to high speed.

"Aah," she kept screaming.

Swishing through the dense forest,the car rammed through hitting the tree and bushes. Kiernan haad completely lost of herself and the car. The headlights went off,and she was steering through complete darkness guided by the little rays of moonlight through the trees.

She hit her head againt the window of a wildly riding car,"huh"she gasped she was withering in pain. Completely scared and helpless.

Though she was partly unconscious,she kept trying to reach for the breaks. She was deep into the woods now,in the deadliest part of the forest. Suddenly she enjoyed a moment of relief when she realised the car had begin slowing down. But it ended soon,when she noticed a cliff.

Kiernan tried hard but knew she wasn't going to be able to stop the car. There was only one thing she coud do now. She reached for the car door but it was jammed a bit. She pushed haed and hit with a 'bang' and at once it opened and she fell out of the moving car. She rolled over sloping land,brushing through the trees,finally landing on hard ground She was badly injured,cuts and bruises,her forehead was bleeding profusely.

From the corner of the eyes,she watched as the car kept moving and fell off through the cliff. It made a loud sound. "Swoosh" battling her wounds, she dragged her body to the edge,she saw the car drowning in the river,she watched helplessly as it sank completely leaving no trace whatsover.

She had tears in her eyes and begin to cry. In a fraction of second,her life had come to an end. She looked to the heavens,"This is it,isn't it? " she wailed in pain knowing that there was no way she'd ever make it out alive.

Kiernan fell to the groung and caught her breath. She knew now,this was the end,she could fell her spirits dying. With great difficulty,she glanced over at the watch on her wrist. It was almost midnight; The 25th of December.

Suddenly she felt the strongest tremors hit her,it ran through her body like a bolt of electric current. Her sense went blank,her body became numb. Her pulse begin dropping rapidly. She breathed heavily trying to hold on to life.

She whispered into the cold air' "Happy birthday to me". No...no happy death day.

She said has she Gasping her breath for last minute.

And with that,she closed eyes and she gave in. She felt nothing. In a few seconds,her heart stopped. Her body lay lifeless on the edge of the cliff.

Terrified, I kept my eyes clamped shut. Whatever caused the agonishing sharp pains in my leg,it was sure it wouldn't look pretty. An overehelming feeling of dread took over and for a moment I thought the pain would only get worse and worse. It took them a moment to gather my thoughts,or at least gather enough of them to think a little clearer.

For half a minute,her body just lay there on the snow. Snowflake in air.

ᑭᑭᑭ

SIX

HANGING TREE

Kiernan got up from unconscious frozen mind with a heavy breath,still confused about the bleeding wounds on her forhead but she walked towards the dark forest and exposed what wass behing it. Through complete darkness a little light lash guided her behind the dark forest.

The Hanging Tree that had a light coming from underneath it filled up the forest with a bright light. She was astonished to see this and her body felt numb with excitement.

Experiencing this as a teenager made her feel more cautious this time,not knwing what could be waiting on the other side, but she coudn't resist the temptation.

And the she saw that there was a light ahead of her;not a few inches away where the back of the woods ought to have been,but a long way off. Somthing cold and cold and soft wa falling on her. She was standing in the middle of a wood at night-time with snow under her feet and snowflakes falling through the air.

She wa feeling courageous to get close to it. She reached out to gently touch it and felt herself being sucked in mid-air,circling around and around just like Alice in wonderland. Her heart raced and she coudn't breathe. All she could remember from the short trip was that she fainted halfway and when she woke up she was in a bed with black clean sheets. She could barely open her eyes as as she still felt dizzy,but she somehow managed to sit up slowly. She looked around the Red and white room with a window to her right and a door to left.

A young petite women entered the room and introduced herself to me.

"My name is ELISA and i am here to help you get better. Here some water she said softly.

I stared at her and smiled weakly for a moment. "Where am I ?" Iasked shakily,pressing my hands against my head.

You dont seem to be from around here. You look different. " She said

She still could not see clearly and did not feel very well so she remained quite. When she didn't respon,Elisa bowed her head,took the empty glass from her hand and left her to rest more.

When i woke up again,I felt much better than earlier and was also ready to start exploring. I walked out of the room and saw a lot of people walking in this long corridor. I noticed they were physically distinct. They had pointy ears,unique hairstyles and colours, like pink or blue hair and all looked muscular or toned.

How are you feeling?' A deep male voice came from behind me asked.

" I turned to look at the most beautiful eyes i had ever seen. His posture made me stretch my neck to its limit as i observed him with my mouth open wide. He moved away s few strands of his silvery-black long hair,tucking it around his pointy ears as he smiled. My nose caught a mesmerising scent coming from him.

I'm... feeling better," I told him breathlessly,my eyes moving down his whole body,obseving his face.

I realised i kept a straight face the whole time,feeling itimidated by his beauty,but it was too late to change my reaction now.

He laughed and said "my name is ROSS DIABOLUS. Welcome to LUMINEERS. I know we alllook strange to you,but don't feel threatened. I found you unconscious at Hanging tree and brought you to our village. Are you the daughter of LILITH ?"

I suddenly came to my senses and realised that i was the one different here.

'No ,i'm Kiernan Shipka, and i'm the daughter of Diana woods. kiernan said

"Your kind is very rare to come by"he said

I knew he could see me blush as my pale skin does not help to hide my red cheeks. I coudn't tlak.

He was so handsome and i was right there,in frount of him looking all messed up. I could feel my hair all over the place and i was in a robe with nothing else to hide.

"Are you ?"

He lifted her up into his arms and towards the room.

"Ssh.....,i wish to taste you. "She started to struggle harder causing him to bite into her soft slim tigh until she stilled. She had struggle longer than most would have been and gasped profusely and shuddering she fell limp on the ground. Softly he moved up to her and gently moved the tangled mass of her plastered on her soft cheek.

Tell me,who owns you? "He snarled again

"You...you do master." She gasped as she pushed at his hips trying to ease some of her pain.

"As her eyes begin to flutter close the last thing she remembered was him pressing a kiss onto her belly.

SEVEN

GIVE ME CHANCE

Kiernan was bride in a blck wedding gown,the dress leaves her shoulder uncovered,instead it's supported around her neck and flows down into a tasteful sqare neckline.

All at once she got her consciousness and shook from her bed sweating face and her body was warm as sulk

When i woke up again, i felt like i was bleeding unconcious. My heart was thumping and screaming for help. Hearing came enterning the room with her wide open.

Aru you alright?" what happend to you?. Elisa asked.

Kiernan took few minutes before she spoke.

It's just a bad dream and where is Diabolus. She inured.

What did you just say? Elisa asked with her eyes open.

didn't you hear me?"Ross Diabolus.

No dont't ever use that name again,Elisa warning her.

But why? is she you master!?" she said

No...no he...is the Devil. Elisa said in fear.

What the fuck are you talking,are you insane,

Of sound mind me,you're new to this place so you don't know about the mgical atmosphere here. Said Elisa laughing.

But i spent my time with him today and he was right here with me.Kiernan said

What the heck are you telling me about? Elisa inured.

Nothing happened to me,thanks for your knindness. Kiernan said smiling.

Please can you do me a favor. Kiernan requested her.

Can you please tell me how to get out of here?" I think i am not one of you,you know thaat.

Please,i'm scared. Kiernan said.

Sorry!" I can't take you but i can show you. Elisa said.

Please show me,i'll just go by nyself,just the place. Kiernan asked

It's uncomplicated,it's dark magical palce with a abig Apple tree!" where thirteen witches were hunged that is why we call it a Hanging tree. Elisa said.

Please just show me the way. Kiernan requesting.

it is perilous. Elisa warned.

Give me a chance. Kiernan asked.

ዖዖዖ

Kiernan carried a lamp with her and Elisa walked slowly as she was scared of entering the forest and Kiernan was still confused about what had happend to her.

Quiet Dead-expect craking woods and grinding winds.

The once smooth network of road thst led to Darkwoodland. SAid Elisa.

i barely detectable beneath layers of dust,said shrubs and leaves. Fallen trees block some of the paths while others continue to grow,their branches no longer prevented from growing into houses. Most doors were either completely gone or mere remnants of rotten wood and rusty metal. The open doorways looked eerie as only darkness showed within. Paint crumbled off of the walls and were slowly peplaced by vines that crawled their way towards the rooftops

Darkwoodland,once a pleasant quiet town and home to friendly folk. Said Elisa.

But now it is an eerie shell of its former self. The wind in the trees and the creaking of wood were the new dominant sound in a once lively community rich in sounds of joy and simple pleasures.

In an almost sick sense of irnony the museum,once home to relics from past discovered and recovered by goddess from around the world,was now once again lost and forgotten. Waiting to be found by those who come next.

You could go anywhere in town you wanted,walk into any home and visit any previously private part of town. Said the Elisa

Black magic assuming it hadn't been destroyed by nature already. But even though everything may seem like it was lost forever there was still a slver lining. While this town was no longer home to the families that lived here,it was now home to families of wild animals.

Kiernan can sense the smell of the forest approaching her and senses her stay till the bitter December snow cold takes full control of her body.

Where does the smell come from? " asked Kiernan.

The hypnotic marliacea is a very rae,tiny plant and can be found in any cold region. It blooms once a year,for two weeks. It has large,needle leaves,which are usually dark red.

it would then disappear for aa whole year and i would start missing it like a heart broken women longing for her lover's embrace. Once bitten twice shy,these days in early winters,as soon as the smell starts to seduce me i try to run away from from it because i know it would soon be gone leaving me high and dry. But how can you escape the seductive devil who is there in every breath you take?" Said Elisa.

Why does it keep snowing here? i see everything is frozen everywhere and i don't understand if it is season or its magical world?. Asked Kiernan.

The day winter turns to summer,a promise shall bring new aggressions and an age of magic. It's always winter in Lumineer---always winter,but it never gets to christmas. Said Elisa

Elisa pointing out her index finger towards the end of the frozen river,fireflies coming through the trees.

The forest was far-reaching,misty, and ancient. Its canopy was eclipsed by yew,elm, and pine,their crowns allowed for short beams of light to descend for bright bushes to use the moist and fertile bottom layer below. Curving tree limbs dropped from most trees,and a mishmash of flowers,which desperately tried to claim and the last ramnants of light,brightened up the otherwise colourless landscape. A mixture of animal noises,predonminantly those of vermin,added life to te forest,and were backed by the occasional roar of a large animal trying to scare away predators.

Okey there we are here,the only reason Devil tree till i die,only to be always longind for his swain smell be careful. Said Elisa.

Kiernan walked slowly towards the end of the river,as she saw a fighure of women behind the woods the breeze caressed her skin with fireflies greeting her around. She walked slowly towards the horror lane bridge. Swiftly turned around to see Elisa but she vanished away tragically and Kiernan was still confused.

Everything hurts. My head hurt.my chest hurt, my feet hurt. What if there was no end to this pain? what if it got worse? these thoughts alone were enough to get my heart racing faster,never mind the pain itself. Several voices echoed through my head. Some telling them everything will be fine,others telling them it won't be. It was difficult to focus between the moments of pain and the voices telling them to stop what they're managed to block out the pain enough to make it nothing more than a minor annoyance. It"ll last a while,but i'll maange. Kiernan talking to herself as she walked over the horror lane river.

EIGHT

SMELL LIKE A TEEN SPIRIT

She begin to walk forword,crunch-chrunching over the horror lane frozen bridge. The snowing and through the wood towards the other light. In about ten minutes she reached it and found it was a lamp-post "with a Weeping Angel" As she stood looking at it,wondering why there was a lamp-post with the statue in the middle of a wood and wondering what to do next. The angel suddenly moved. Sttarted,she immediately stepped back. The angel changed her posture! she coudn't move for a second,mesmerised by the strange sight,Wondering what was going on. She finally gathered courage to move closer and see what the angel was like up close.

The angel changed her posture again!. It had four wings,two broad and two narrow. All of sudden a goblin attack came out from behind the wood,leaving no chance for the angel to defend itself. A loud thud was heard. I fainted at the moment but woke up feeling like a dead women.

When i woke up i was on the rooftop of,. The Gravehill ice prison of graveyard castle was Thirteen narrow,firm walls made of dark green stone. Rough windows are scattered generously and the walls in seemingly perfect symmentry,along with small hoes for archers and artillery. A regular gate with massive wooden doors along and a moat offers a warm haven within these cold,Isloated landsand it's the only way in,at least to those unfamiliar with the castle and its surroundings. Large boulders litter the fields outside the castle,paths to and from the castle snake around them and farm plots are small ans scattered all around. This castle has clearly stood the test of time and its inhabitants are intent on making sure it stays that way for ages to come.

The black canines guarding the door with a very short,thick,warped blade made of ceramic is held by a grip wrapped in extremely rare,deep orange buffalo skin. With its sharp,dual-edged blade this weapon is the champion's choice. It'll crush your enemies with cleaving hacks and piercing stabs. The blade has a jagged,curled cross-guard,creating the ideal weight balanced to allow for smooth and accurate swings with the blade. The cross-guard has a decorative claw on each side, this weapon wasn't created by just any blacksmith.

A blade itself is bare. No markings,no decorations and no rngravings,but the blade will surly be decorated in battle. This weapon is used by the royal guard. You'd expect nothing less from such fighters.

A wolf creature he had cold eyes and was holding my guardian angle's torn wings in his hands. Beldam came walking with her magic sceptre. One of the goblins opened the door and he grabbed me into his arms by pulling towards the front lane towards the door,which was made of iron and titanium. And i saw Rosina crow with magical spectre. This wand is made out of Elder wood,which heavily favours those with an affinity for spoken magic. The handle is made out of Blackthorn wood, which in turn often prefers those with strong family roots. However,the combination of this strand of Elder wood and Blackthorn wood means the wand will seek out somebody with an incredible destiny.

Who is the matriarch coven of the faery tree of Lumineers and her Horn orcs.

She said,thid justice for the young girl will not be in vain. She smeels like a young teen. Wives of the divine of children of night.

Dr. Grave was a mad scientist who looks can be deceiving when dealing with Rosina crow,but the fact he's opportunistic and angry is just the tip of the iceberg. There's the fact he's also disorderly,difficult and imprudent,but fortunately they're mixed with behaviours of being exciting as well. But focus on him as this is what he's pretty much infamous for. Even the best intentions have been soured because of this and his greed,which is a true shame for both sides.

Fair is fair theough, Dr. Graves has some endearing sides. He's courageous and observant among others,it could be worth taking a chance just once. Unfortunately his anger is always there to ruin everything again. Placed the wings on her backbone and she turned into maleficent women who was merely a beautiful women and she smiled softly laughing at Kiernan like a malocchio. And the prophecy of the Gravehill kingdom was; I swiftly turned to a senseless,

A dragon climbing on the wall behind me. That's impossible! Dragons don't exist in reality, so it would be impossible to see one climbing on a wall. Dark azure eyes sit delicately within the creature's rounded,thorny skull,which gives the creature a vicious looking appearance.

Two crystal growths sit atop its head,just above its thick,Warped ears. A row of small crystal growths runs down the sides of each on its jaw lines. Its nose is flat and has two long,angular nostrils and there are horns on its chin. Several sharp teeth poke out from the side of its mouth and reveal only a fraction of the terror hiding inside.

A sharp neck runs down from ts head and into a snake-like body. The top is covered in warped scale and rows of crystal growth run down its spine. Its bottom is covered in stone-like scales and is colored slightly darker than the rest of its body. Four musclear limbs carry its body and allow the creature to stand noble and imposing. Each limb has three digits, each of which end in strong nails seemingly made of obsidian.

Terrifying wings grow starting from its shoulders and end all the way down at its pelvis. The wings are almost demonic,the inner sides of the wing are full of minor holes and sharp,spiky scales cover the top of each visible bone.

Its narrow tail ends in a curved talcon and is covered in the same warped scales as its body.

Who is the Dirdar,Lord of ice squealer!!

I dont feel comfortable with her anymore. She has a divine presence upon the day the mark is revealed,a contract shall cause a new life and a reunion of enemies. When it comes that the moon turns red, a random act of kindness shall usher forth the overthrowing of royalty. When the moment comes that prey kills the kings of all the kingdom's,a secret women shall bring forth an end to enemies and a vivious war. When the moment comes that the world turns to winter,an ecchange of coins shall bringe forth a reunion of enemies. Said Dirdar.

Dr. Grave's fairly long sleeved,animal skin jacket covers him well above his groyne and is barely tied with string at the left side. The sleeves of his jacket are very wide and reach down to below his hands,they're decorated with a decorstive band alomst at the edges. The jacket has a narrow v-neck which reveals part of the modest shirt worn below it and is worn with a long cloth belt,which is held together by an ornate pin. The cloth belt is sightly decorative,but mostly there to hang things from. His pants are simple and a loose fit and reach down to his furred dhoes. The shoes are made from a are fur,but are otherwise not any different from others. Looking at the sidewalks around the women. Kiernan who was gyrating her head towards the Dragons she was still confused about the place which was a beautiful magical castle.

Polished brsziers attached to each of the fourteen marbel columns light up every part of the throne hall and shroud it in a dark orange radiance. The angelic paintings on the embowed ceiling dance in the flickering light while carved images and statuettes lookdown upon the granite floor of this lavish hall. A verdigris runs down from the throne for few metres before coming to an end while square dag banners with burnished quilting hang from the walls. Between each banner, many of them have been lit and in turn illuminate the artistic potrayals of late royal family members below them. Narrow,stained glass windows of mesmerising mosaics are shrounded by veils coloured the same verdigris as the banners. The curtains have been adorned with jewels and emblazoned edges. A lavish throne of sapphire sits atop a balcony overlooking the throne hall and is adjoined by two smaller and less elabrate seates foor visiting royalty of other nations. The throne is covered in byzantine images and fixed on each of the ornate legs is a crystal animal head. The bulky pillows are a light verdigris and these too have been adorned with golden needlework. Has Dragon moving gyrating around the throne hall.

A short neck runs down from its head and into a snake-like body. The top is covered in warped scales and row of crystal growth run down its spine. Its bottom is covered in stone-like scales and is coloured slightly darker than the rest of its body. Four muscular limbs carry its body and allow the creture to stand noble and imposing. Each limb has tree digits,each of which end in strong nails seemingly made of obsidian.

Terrifying wings grow starting from its shoulders and end all the way down at its pelvis. The wings are almost demonic,the inner sides of the wing are fully of minor holes and sharp,spiky scales cover the top of each visible bone.

Its narrow tail ends in a curved talon and is covered in the same warped scales as its body.

Those listening to their royal highness can do so on the countless slightly illuminated alder benches,all of which are facing the throne in a half circle. Those of higher stanging can instead takes seats in the humble looking balconies overlooking the hell. Has Dragon moving gyrating around the throne hall.

The werewolves marched towards the Throne hall,with a small,wide,jagged blade made of adamantium held by a grip wrapped in lavish,red deerskin. The shield's edges are reinforced with thick metal metal plating and have been decorated with inscribed runes.

Listen to them,the children of the night. What music they make!. Be my guest,said the Rosina crow.

Kiernan was tragically dragged by commander of werewolves Rex,to Dragontooth Regional prison. She felt pain in her chest, she felt pain in her arms and she felt pain in her mind. Desperate for some form of relief she sought out every solution. Which was the end of mysteries of life and she was still confused.

NINE

PRISONER LOVE

When i found that i was a prisoner a sort of wild feeling came over me. I rushed up and down the stairs,trying every door and peering out of every window i could find,and i found cerberus guarding the door behind and i was helplessness overpowered all other feelings. When i look back after a few hours i think i must have been mad for the time,for i behaved much as a rat does in a trap.

The prison cell was barely six feet four. The walls were the same thick grey stone as the dwellings of the region,but instead of a wide window with a flower box there was a mean barred opeing with thick metal bars and no glass. In the summer the fresher air was a relief,helping to alleviate the stench of festering sewage but in the cold seasons it let in a wicked draft and reduced the temperature to near freezing. It was no brighter inside than the gathering gloom of dusk,even at middy. The bed was a plank of wood on legs,there was no mattress,no cushioning and only one thin blanket. It was either suffocatingly quiet or pierced with the screams of tortured inmates.

When,however,the Goblins had come to me that i was helpless i sat down quietly,as quietly as i have ever done anything in my life,and began to think over what was best to be done. I am thinking still,and as yet have come to no definite conclusion.

Fightin's for dogs!" He roared,smashing a fist twice the size of a normal man's against the rusty bars. He stopped the makeshift blade on the ground,before casting another,even angrier look around. His eyes came to rest on me,and the blood on my cheek.

Does the princess need lessons in making friends?" He said, in a sharp,vicious tone. I watched as he lent over to pick up and examine the blade and soon i found him towering over me. I saw the attacker,the man who had whittled the makeshift knife and slashed our cellmate,rise to claim responsibility. Out of sight of the imposing figure, who's malicious gaze was fixed on my face,i raised a hand and gestured for him to stay quiet.

He ate that rat that kept coming into the cage."

'Hornball?" I exclaimed. I glanced a look over to the bleeding member of our pack of caged men,he too was clutching his knief wound with a pained expression. "I hope that hurts!"

Bolo sat beside me. " You can see the way we look up to you,right? how every one of us lokks up to you"

"Stop." I moaned,i knew where this was going.

"We'll follow you. All you have to do is lead. We can take our home bck,i know it."

" I can't do it." I breathed with a fragile note. " So many would die. If not us all. I cannot bear the idea of costing one man his life,let alone hundreds."

"Life? what life is this?" Bolo gestured around the cage. Men in rags slung up against bars. Bruised,malnourished and dishevelled. "I remember what life was like before this. It's all i cling to."

"You know i would gladly give my life for this place to be free, Bolo. But not theirs."

Two suns rose and set before i did anything else other than eat,sleep and relieve myself through the bars of my cast-iron-prison. I dreamt nightly of being free of this place. Away from it all. It was all i wanted. I didn't want to fight. I didn't want to rebel. I just wanted to be free. The grey clouds has started to clear,and the cold sea air was starting to warm just a little bit.

I saw a strange man on the wall behind me. Uside down that's impossible! so it would be impossible to hang on a wall. I swiftly turned and stepped backwards. Who is the vampire hanging on the wall? i noticed there was no one there.

It wasn't as if Kiernan had planned on being locked in a basement. No windows. It wasn't like he'd turn into a bat because he coudn't do that,but he could make them think he wasn't there. Or at least he hoped that was true,considering he had no idea who had locked him away.

She thought about the count of Asher Dracula.

How did i escape? with difficulty. How did i plan this moment? with pleasure.

But unlike,Kiernan didn't have a mad priest to show him the way to treasure so that he could get reveenge on his captor and win back the women he loved.

Kiernan though about the women he loved for a bit. Did she love him? or was she rejecting him simply because he was a vampire ahd she was not? or was he just thinking about it way too much.

It would have been nice to be back in his own comfortable home, playing the piano,enteraining friends or curled up in a chair with a good book and a nice goblet of wine or blood or...

A sudden noise brought him out of his his reverie. A brick popped out of the wall and a pale hand came through. What could this sudden event of fate mean? was she to be rescued?

He reached for the hand. It pulled back at his touch.

'You're like ice," hissed a quiet voice.

"I run a little cold.Who are you.?

"I am but a prisoner of love'.

Kiernan took a deep breath,at least a deep one for a vampire. Why did he always find himself in situation like this with someone who was bat shit crazy?

"Where are we and why? no stupid answer"

he answered with silence. That wouldn't do' kiernan went to the whole in the wall and looked through. It was drak but he could see a slight shadow."Answer me, Where are we ?Do you know?"

Something jumped on his lap and shook him awake. Kiernan took his book (The Count of Asher Dracula)

And he dropped the Magical Ring and nearly tipped over the floor. A small black kitten curled up and started to purr. What a crazy dream. What a srange and bizarre dream he did'nt have have a Black kitten .

sitting still and quiet Kiernan listened for noise of a vistior. He'd hear the slightest breath or an exicted heart beat . If they were clode enough he'd smell blood

There was no other living thing in the room expect Kiernan and the kitten .

"Where did you come from dear kitty?

The kitten only purred. She was tiny, maybe eight weeks old at the most. A sense of unease overcame him. Making his fangs ready he stood and turned around. Standing behind him was pale from-A woman she held her out hand.

"I am but prisoner of love" She whispered

"Is this you're cat?"

But Kiernan never got his answer. He vanished in a wisp of smoke with the smell of sulphur.

What is it with Vampire and cats love? The unsusepecting spirit laughed then said aloud, " if you're going to hunt my dreams and my throne you might as well tell me who you are"

Kiernan felt a cold blast of air then heard a soft laugh then the soft sound of a woman's voice"when you compare the sorrows of real life to the pleasure of the imaginary onr, you will never want to live again,Only to dream forever." Unseeable spirit

Children from The count of Asher Dracula. Voice fainted

A prisoner of love. " Not me," thought Kiernan, " not me."

When Kiernan looks at the magical Ring in her hand. Is this one thing that will help to get out of the place and go back home?,take her to the future and she puts the Ring. All of a sudden she is transported to a whole new universe.

ᑭᑭᑭ

TEN

END OF THE WORLD

Care for it as it were your own, or watch it melt to ash and bone. Words that echoed in mymind as i edged my way through the forest. The trees were spread sparse,and lay bare. Their dark,silvery trunks clinging to the ground through exposed roots:roots thst wove their way across the grim,grey dirt. I had to be careful not to trip as i walked,the entire forest floor was laden with them.

The air was still. Not a sound floated through it, save the crunch of my boots on the dry,dead ground. And that's what this place was, or at least seemed: dead. There was no colour,no life. The forest seemed empty,devoid of anythung you might expect to see in a woodland. No animals, no water, no sunlight breaking its way through the canopy. The lack of leaves would have left the whole forest to bathe in the warm glow of the sun,were it not hidden beneath prepetual clouds.

I came to a steeply crested dirt mound. Either side were trees,jagged roots and felled decaying logs. It seemed to be my only way forward. In my attempts to scramble up, i lost my footing and fell forward. I wasn't quite sure how, my foot felt planted one second,then as if the ground was gone the next,but it didn't matter. I had made it over the rise but landed on my stomach in the dirt. Peeling upright as quickly as i could, i frantically checked my pocket. To my relief,there was no harm done. My Ring was safe. Dusting myself off, i continued onwards,heading deeper into the forest.

Nasty isn't it..."

I flew around, a haunting voice catching me by surprise. My heart in my mouth,my breath caught in my lungs, i found myself peering down at a hagged old women,head spun with dry and curling white hairs. She sat against the base of a tree,wore a tattered olg white dress down to her feet,no shoes and a crooked smile.

"To be caught off-guard by a scary old women in the middle of a forest" she continued, her smile broadening. I nodded frantically in agreement.

"What brings you out here?" she pressed. "Alone".

Her expression was warm but her eyes were cold. They were like the forest around me.

lifeless and empty.

"Nothing".

"Nothing?" she replied,sceptically. " I doubt that very much."

"What are you doing out here?" I asked, trying to turn the conversation to her.

"Hmm? Oh, just sitting."

'Sitting?"

We looked at each other, an eeire smile on her face,what i imagined to be nerves on mine.

" I better head this way," I said after a pause,edging away from her.

"Oh yes,you better have." The old women croaked. " it'll be getting dark soon."

I nodded awkwardly at her,scurrying away. Before i could move out of earshot, i heared her call.

'Must be very valuable,whatever is in your pocket."

I turned back to answer,to lie or question her knowledge of what lay beneath the fabric of my clothes,but there was nobody to respond back to. The women was gone.

With every hair on my body standing on end, i carried on. I had to be there soon, or must at lwast be getting close.She was right,though,it was getting darker. It was impossible to know high the sun was in the sky. Between myself and the clouds was a high floating mist that wafted through the treetops. It scattered what little light crept its way through the clouds,destroying all indication of the placement of the sun within the sky. All i knew was, i was losing light. I shuddered at the thought of being caught out here in the dark. Waking to a wrinkled old crone standing over me, fumbling at my pocket and scared me half to death. She'd already done that once,i suppose if she came back and did the other half she'd finifh the job.

I could feel the fear etching its way into my body. A strange sensation of heat on my skin, despite the cold. A feeling of movement in my stomach,without any food inside it. And a distortion behind my eyes;the world was the same as how i alays knew it,but somehow looked different at the same time. Like i was seeing more detail,my unconscious mind was looking for things it normally wouldn't. Like creepy old ghost women.

I didn't want to be here anymore.

The only way out was forward. I amrched on,watching my footsteps carefully. I would seemingly trip every time i looked up, like the roots beneath me were tricking my eyes.

Where i thought was clear was suddenly not. This forest was shapeless,aimless, it just kept going. But then,my heart sank,as i came to familiar sight. A crested dirt ,ound,this time with scrapped boot marks down the rise. I approached it cautiously. To either side were trees,felled logs and jagged roots. There was no mistake it. Carefully,i climbed,watching my feet as i went. With a hop i sprang over the ridge and immediatly cast my eyes around the trees,turning back to check for old,haggard strangers. But there was nobody.

"Nasty isn't it..."

I gasped as a jolt of shock struck me deep with in my chest.

"To be caught off-guard twice by a scary women".

Slowely, i turned back around. There she was,standing barefoot in the dirt. Hunched over,neck twisted,peering up at me through the spirals of hair falling down her face.

"What's going on?" i demanded,eyes darting around the forest for other potential surprises. The women had not been there mere moments ago,and the trees were spred so far apart around us that there was no way she could have appeared from behind one of them.

"I would like to see the treasure you carry". She softly,wearing the same broad smile.

"It is not for you," i said,trying to strike my tone with some form of confidence while carefully shielding my pocket with my hands.

The women's smile dropped to a sneer. She folded the hair out of her face to reveal a harsh and angry expression,yet those eyes held nothing but emptiness. No emotion,nothing. "There is only one reason people vistit this forest. Only one reason they travel so deep".

"Get away from me,crone!" i wailed,sprinting round her,my hands still covering my pockets. I ran deeper into the the forest,zig-zagging between the gnarled roots as fast as i could. I kept the pace for as long as i could,constantly switching between tracking my movement across the floor-careful not to trip-and looking up for signs of repetition. Eventually,after a fairly lengthy,yet cautious run, i started to tire. I wasn't the most physically fit of individuals. I came from wealth,i didn't have to be.

Panting,exausted and pleading with my own head for signs of the creature that i sought, i came upon a particularly dangerous looking patch of roots,stretching ahead of me into the far distance. They spunup in all directions,curved and twisted,some even looping twice over before burying themselves back into the ground. It seemed like they were fleeing the very earth itself.

I looked around the desolate landscape. No sign of women,or crests or anything familiar;except a brutally grey and unappealing forest. I broke off my pace and opted for a slow walk through the entangled roots. Eyes firmly at my feet,i made steady progress for all of thirty seconds,then i glanced up.

There it was. The crested dirt mound. Right before my eyes. How? what had happend to the swarming roots? There was no way I'd made my way through them. Shaking,but with anger and fear.i put my hand forward and climbed. Eyes darting about the place,i kept myself moving,circling as i went,looking for the old women. I didn't want to be surprised again.

But she wasn't here. I couldn't see her anywhere. I stood for a good few minutws,in the dead silence of the forest. Waiting for her to appear. She didn't come. I could feel my mind slipping away from me. I was becoming desperate. The sun didn't appear to be moving. It was still fading,and had been for what seemed like hours. I couldn't see a way put. How could i escape a forest thst could change its shape at a moment's notice? nobody had warned me this forest played games with you. That a witch lived between its deathly edges and tangled roots.

Slowely,i reached into my pocket and pulled out my ring. And i lay in my palm. I held it out before me, gazing at its smooth shell. I felt a coldness behind me. Not a breeze,more like that cold feeling of placing your hand near frozen water. An aura.

The women appeared. Shuffling past my shoulder,she came to a kneel in front of me.. Again she wore that same smile. Again her eyes were lifeless.

"Leave it here,and i'll let you go". She wispered,eyes still fixed uopn the striking little shining ring.

"I know what happens if i let go of it". I whimperd. I was afraid,but not more afraid than i was of dying,cold and alone in this forest.

"Do it". She urged.

"Go on. Take it from me." I said, a pleading note clear in my quivering voice.

"Just put it on the ground." The witch breathed with a gesture towards the floor.

"Why don't you just take it?"

"Put it on the ground." She was becoming agitated again. The smile wiped from her face. Her anger was building. "Put it on the ground and leave!"

I watched her a moment,wondering why she woudn't just take the ring. Then,cautiously,i reached out with one hand. As i slid my hand towards her skin,it floated away like mist. She really was a ghost;an apparition.

"You have no power here," i said under my breath. You can't do anything to me."

" I can trap you in this place until you're too weak to carry on." The witch screeched at me. "I'm giving you a chance to leave her alive."

But the weels were turing in my mind. I was starting to piece it together. What was happening. Not how it eas happening,mind,that part still eluded me,but what was causing my confusion,my lost sense of direction and inability to avoid the crested dirt mound. I could see the witch growing anxious,she twitched as she crouched before me, watching me intently.

"you can only control what i cannot see," i said finally,cracking a small smile.

She gazed at me,blankly for a moment,seemingly lost for words. When she spoke,she didn't say what i thought she might. She didn't question what i knew,she didn't ask me why or how i'd figured it out. No,instead,in the softest,and weakest of voices,she just said:"please don't.

I rose quickly. I kept my eyes on the horizon and i walked onwards,straight through her. I did not let my vision waiver from the direction in which i walked. I stumbled, i tripped and fell. Cut, bled and bruised. But she couldn't trap me if i didn't take my eyes off the path.

" Wait!" i heard her voice behind me. "Look"!

"No!" i called out, not turning my head even an inch.

I had a newfound sense of confidence. I'd beaten her magic and her tricks. I felt a surge of energy within my body,my fear turning to determination. From behind a tree ahead of me,she came into view. She appeared to be sobbing,or at least, sad. I refused to look at her directluy,my eyess were looking nowhere but dead ahead. As i walked past her,she started to scuttle along beside me.

"Please!" she begged. "Please. Drop the ring and leave. You are making a mistake."

"This is my task. This is how i look after my family." I replayed firmly,shaking off her feeble attempts to sway my decision and pull me off course.

"I cannot take it anymore. Please,don't do thi-" But she was cut short. We'd arrived. I had been so close for so long.

Before me was clearing in the forest. Within it lay a deep crater entrenched by roots and fallen trees;within the crater itself,was what i set out to find. The creature hummed softly. A low, baritone noise. It was an almost perfect half-sphere,about the size of a small cottage,sitting dead centre, in the heart of the crater. Its skin was a harsh pink mixed with tinges of brown,and all over its body were placed long,barbed spikes. It reminded me of a more jagged looking sea urchin;a delicacy we often treated ourself back home. It had no face,eyes,nose or anything else you'd normally associate with an animal. I supposed they may be under its striking shell.

A quick glance at witch told me she was devastated by my find. She shrank down onto all fours,clutching the lip of the crater,looking down on the otherworldly beast in the pit below.

"I can't..."She moaned. "I can't go through this again. Please don't make me"

"It is not for me to help you," I replied harshly,fed up with the trickster's tatics. "I am here for a reason,and i will see it through".

.

The witch was gone.

A few minutes after it began,it all stopped. In that time,the crater had grown,the roots had leapt further from the earth and trees had fallen into the pit all around us. The creature itself was much larger as well. Its vivid red and orange skin returned to its normal pink state. Again,it was humming softly. I stood,watching the animal. Waiting for what i knew must come next. It had to...it couldn't not. It took some time,time enough for me to grow increasingly nervous,but eventually,the gaint started to convulse in and out again,as it very slowely crept away from me.

Sitting on the lip of the enormous pit,i wiped the slim off gem with my clothes. It was a perfect circle,a glowing blue pearl. The sizee of my cupped hands,it shone without any light reflecting into it. I couldn't have asked for anything so stunning. This gem was perhaps the most valuable single item anyone could get their hands on right now,and it would keep my family in great wealth for a century.

I left the forest,nearly skipping,overjoyed. The gem was hidden beneath my clothes,i couldn't let anyone know i had it. Not until it and i were saftely home. Nobody but the inner circle of my family knew of this place. If anyone were to discover it,our fortune would be ripped from brnrath us. Soon, i came to the crested mound,but this time i was facing the other way.

"I used to be young and beautiful,you know." The witch was waiting for me,on the other side of the crest. Some of her silver hair had fallen out since was last met. She looked more wrinkled,was hunched over in a cruel arch and spoke with a very weak and croaking voice. " You've taken this all from me."

"Everything must have an end". I replied,matter of factly,now very much unafraid of the deathly figure before me.

"And what will you do when i'm gone. When will this be gone?" she gestured to the forest around her. Decay hung in air,the trees were looking wilted,the bark of the roots cracking." I cannot take much more."

"I don't care," I said honestly. "What i care about is getting what i need right now. And i have what i need. You're still here,aren't you? The forest still stands. We'll try and give you longer to heal this time...maybe that will keep you going a little longer."

"It's not enough." The end of the world. She sobbed.

"That's all i can give you." And with that,i left. And kKiernan puts the ring. All of a sudden she is transported to a whole new universe from her. Hoping i would never hear from her or see her again. Somebody else would have to come back here,of course,but i wasn't going to be me. I'd be long dead.

ቃቃቃ

ELEVEN

THE NEW BEGING

Hundreds of thousands have withstood very sunny weather over the years for a once-in-a-lifetime experience,and tanning in layers,lay off the booze and bring some sun warmers. All the people gathered around the beach.

The city of Foxburgh was built at the base of a rugged mountain and is truly a future oriented urban phenomenon. Its elegance is matched by the backdrop of green,fertile fields which have helped shape the city to what it is today. The riches these fields brought were of great importance,but they were also influential when it came to architecture designs as the vast majority of buildings are slim and tall,which mimics the grasses and openness of the fields around them.

Kiernan was confused about the place where all the people gathered around the beach and the sea. She had never seen anything like it and didn't know what to expect. And she saw some women in bikinis and dancing with mens who had their own music. She couldn't believe her eyes.

The skyline is spinkeled with peculiar skyscrapers and they have aspects which represent their past,present and future. Science and development is flourishing in Foxburgh and it has attracted a lot of attention. Many different cultures have left their mark not just on trade and relations,but also upon the city's identity. What historically was a city of few differences has grown into a new culture of variety and it's this that unites the one million people to this day.

As i lay on the minute golden grains of sand,i looked up at the brilliant sky, adorned with flashes of pink and orange and purple,Mirroring the colours of a flawless seasoned apricot. The goddess-like sun's face is being embraced bt the demure navy fingertips of the skyline.

The dull light of the sun somehow manages to kindle my senses in a way i had never seen or felt before. Everything felt like one in a painting. The waves break gently into white foam on the black beach. The small crystals in the sand glimmer and twinkle brilliantly against the sunrays. The seagulls ride with the wind and the soft sand cushions my toes.

All of a sudden someone tapped at me on my shoulder and i was shocked to discover that i was still alive in the world.

Black,straight hair is pulled back to reveal a full,radiant face. Dancing hazel eyes,set tightly within their body,watch lovingly over the mines they've stood guard for so long.

A beard gracefully compliments his hair and cheeksbones and leaves a pleasant memory of his fortunate destiny.

This is the face of Ross Diabolus, a true devil's lover among humans. He stands alluringly among others,despite his tough frame.

There's something bewildering about him,perhaps it's a feeling of indifference or perhaps it's simply his clumsiness. But nonetheless,girls tend to shower him with gifts, while wishing they were more like him.

Excuse me. Said the Ross.

As i entered the club behind Ross Diabolus i was stunned by the New world of debauchery i was entering. It was a huge space filled with people,flashing lights,loud music,and all kinds of dancing. The best viberation off the walls as you entere the admission doors;the crowd is out in force and ready to party. The drinks are flowing across the tables just as fact as the bartenders can make them,conversation is loud and patriots are struggling to hear over the thumping music and the dance floor is filled with sweaty bodies swaying to the beat.

Kiernan groaned as she moved her head to the side,the things she was lying on which she was amused was a pillow. Was soft like cotten.

She peeled her eyes, slowly adjusting the light surrounding.

Why am i here?" she asked herself confused as to why. in a man bedroom in different clothes than she wore in the past.

Ah,you see a little mate of mine and you aren't going anywhere,you will never be out of gasp. Ross with smirk on his lips.

And he left me alone in the room and he walked out of the door behind me. And as i heard him go, i began to cry,for i knew all too well that i'd been left behind.

Kiernan swiftly turned. She wondered why she was casting two shadows. Afterall, there was only a single lightbulb. All at once she heard a loud thud noise in the window,the grinning face stared at me from the darkness beyond my bedroom windows.

As she stood behind the wall,closing her eyes, she woke up to hear knocking on glass. At first, i thought it was the window until i heard it come from the mirror again.

As she saw a women spirit figure in the mirror and she was stretching her hands towards Kiernan,stopped and backed up to the wall behind.

Stay away from me! what do you want?

The reflection simply let out to mute laugh, before her expression went back to being black. She lifted her hand up and gave one little twitching of her finger.

The mirror smashed into millions little shards and all that was left was Kiernan screaming.

Now you must stay here in my place,until someone breaks the mirror again the new beginning. Said the spirit.

All the sudden Kiernan hauled into the broken mirror like air being sucked into the room with a black smoke burning women screaing.

ᐅᐅᐅ

TWELVE

TIME TO SLEEP

Carefully opening the package,Asher discovered a formerly unknown packet of love letters between Dinna woods, unknown to the modern world. Everyone back then had know,well almost everyone who knew the couple. They were just too polite to sy anything.

The paper was till in good condition and the ink strong. "Very good,"he said to himself. Dealing in old documents and antiques could be tricky if you didn't know what was real and what was not. He always knew what was real.

As he gently lifted the old letter back into the box there was a sudden flas of light and a beautiful women in jeans and a sweater suddenly appeared before him.

"Asher? Darling,what are you doing here?" the women seemed surprised to see him. Well damn,he was equally surprised. It was almost 3:00 a.m. and her shop was closed for the Thanksgiving holiday week.

He looked her up and down. Tall,pretty,sort of out of place. No, really out of place. "this is my place of business. Do i know you?"

"You're...are you a tie traveller too? you did't tell me.

Asher was not amused. "What are you talking about? what is this Dinna?"

She stepped towards him and smiled that dazzling smile of hers again. "How did you get here?"

She took another step forward. "Then how did you go from being in 2313 back to 2024?

"So i know you in the future?"

"We're lovers. Don't you remember?"

He didn't remember. But it suddenly dawned on him where she had come from and why she was there. " I haven't been there yet'"he quietly told her.

She wasn't the first time traveller he'd run across in his 465 years,but this is the first time he'd encountered her.

"What is your name?" He asked her he stepped closer.

"Kiernan. How could you know?"

"This is as far as i've come my dear. I can't travel to the future."

She looked confused. " You're in the past,Asher."

"My present. You don't know,do you? in the future we're still hiding who we really are. Kiernan,are we in a relationship of the heart or is just a physical thing?"

Her eyes watered up. Asher, don't do this."

Kiernan,do you know what i am?

"You're the man i'm falling in love with."

"I'm the man who will take what he needs and either leave you or kill you. My advice would be to change time let me be".

A tear rolled down her beautiful face. "No. How did you get here."

"The question should be how did i i get THERE. Kiernan went back to sleep." He whispered her name and stepped closer. "I'm sorry it has to be this way."

He kissed her then moved to her neck. He could taste unknown drugs of the future in her system,no doubt somthing to help with the effects of time travels always had memories that were confusing and somewhat ignorant. What they knew of the past was almost always based on fantasy and what they wanted it ot be,not what it really had been.

Looking down on the sleeping women,Asher thought that she must be intelligent to be part of a Time Travel program,but emotionally she was like a teenage girl all full of fluttery ideas and dreams of romance. He'd never fall in love with her. She wasn't of his kind and she never would be.

Yawning,he looked at the clock to realise dawn was almost here. Time to sleep. " I'm the ultimate time traveller. A Vampire dear. I only go forward. Until we meet again." Then he kissed her gently and left her alone to return to her own time and his future.

Printed by Libri Plureos GmbH in Hamburg,
Germany